THE COMPLETE big NATE

THE COMPLETE big NATE

by LINCOLN PEIRCE

VOLUME I

Andrews McMeel Publishing®
a division of Andrews McMeel Universal

WHAT'S OUR NEXT PLAY?
LOOK! OVER THERE!
THOSE GIRLS ARE WATCHING US!
OOOOH! THEY ARE, AREN'T THEY?
LET'S GIVE THEM A SAMPLE OF OUR AWESOME FOOTBALL SKILLS!
YOU THROW ME A BOMB, AND I'LL MAKE AN INCREDIBLE GRAB!
THEN YOU RUN DOWNFIELD TO MEET ME, AND WE CELEBRATE WITH A THUNDEROUS "HIGH-FIVE!"
HIKE!
TOSS!
YES!
Peirce
THUD!
A RIGHTY SHOULD NEVER TRY TO "HIGH FIVE" A LEFTY.....
ARE THEY STILL WATCHING?

BRAND NEW YEAR!
Last year I was always getting in trouble with Mrs. Godfrey because she totally hated my guts. But I have decided that this year will be different.
In all my years of teaching I yak YAK yak yak
I am going to try to butter her up. I am going to try to get on her good side. I know it sounds disgusting, but if it means less detention, it will be worth it.
Detention
Sigh.
Tick tick tick
If I pull this off, I will be a genius. I think my plan will work because I am getting help from one of the all-time greats in this area.
How to be a teacher's PET
"GOOD MORNING, MRS. GODFREY. WOULD YOU CARE FOR AN APPLE?"
NO, NO, NO! SAY IT WITH FEELING!
Peirce

"GOOD MORNING, MRS. GODFREY."... "GOOD MORNING, MRS. GODFREY..."
"GOOD MORNING, MRS. GODFREY."... "GOOD MORNing, MRS. GODFREY."...
"GOOOOD MORNING, MRS. GODFREY!" "GOOD MORNING, MRS. GODFREY."...
GOOD MORNING, NATE.
GOOD MORNING, MRS. GODZILLA!
Peirce

TEACHERS LOVE BEING COMPLIMENTED! WATCH ME AND DO WHAT I DO!
RIGHT!
GOOD MORNING, MRS. GODFREY!
GOOD MORNING, BOYS.
YOU LOOK VERY PRETTY THIS YEAR, MRS. GODFREY!
YEAH! YOU LOOK A LOT LESS FAT!
WHY DON'T WE TAKE OUR SEATS, NATE?
DID YOU HAVE LIPOSUCTION OVER THE SUMMER OR WHAT?
Peirce

YOU WANT TO GET ON GODFREY'S GOOD SIDE? VOLUNTEER TO ANSWER A QUESTION!
GOTCHA!
CAN ANYONE TELL ME THE ANSWER TO NUMBER THREE?
OOH! OOH! ME! ME!
YES, NATE?
I DON'T KNOW!
WE HAVE TO TALK.
THAT WAS EASY! I SHOULD HAVE STARTED THIS STUFF YEARS AGO!
Peirce

TODAY'S OUR FIRST TEST OF THE YEAR! HERE'S WHERE ALL MY BROWN-NOSING FINALLY PAYS OFF!
BEING NICE TO GODFREY ALL WEEK HAS BEEN MURDER, BUT IF I ACE THIS TEST, IT'S **WORTH** IT!
DID YOU STUDY?
STUDY? WHO NEEDS TO STUDY? I'VE BEEN BUTTERING HER UP FOR FIVE DAYS! SHE'LL GIVE ME AN "A" FOR JUST SHOWING UP!
I CAN FEEL MY GRADES CHANGING ALREADY!
SO CAN I...
Peirce

TRYING TO GET ON GODFREY'S GOOD SIDE ISN'T WORKING! SHE STILL DOESN'T LIKE ME!
GIVE IT TIME!
NO! FORGET IT, FRANCIS! LET'S FACE IT, THE WOMAN HATES ME! SHE'S ALWAYS HATED ME, AND SHE STILL HATES ME!
NATE, I'VE DECIDED TO MAKE YOU MY "BLACK-BOARD MONITOR" FOR THE MONTH OF SEPTEMBER!
PAT! PAT!
SEE?
NO, YOU DON'T GET IT! THAT'S GOOD!
Peirce

OH BOY! A PACKAGE!
WRIGHT
HMM... SOME KIND OF FREE SAMPLE...
"E-Z DO-IT-YOURSELF PERM KIT! MAKE YOUR HAIR BEAUTIFUL IN THE PRIVACY OF YOUR HOME!"
I'D LOVE TO PERM MY HAIR... MY HAIR IS SO BORING...
I COULD TRY ONE OF THESE KITS, BUT WHAT IF I DID IT WRONG? I'D LOOK LIKE AN IDIOT!
IF ONLY I COULD PRACTICE DOING IT FIRST! IF ONLY I HAD A HEAD OF HAIR THAT I COULD....
!
STRANGE.... I JUST FELT A CHILL....
OH, NAAAATE!
Peirce

Mr. Rosa!
Being back in school stinks, except for ART class, with my favorite teacher MR. ROSA.
OPEN UP to your creative side, for petes SAKE!
I do not WAnt to brag or anything, but I am probably Mr. Rosa's best student because of my wicked art skills. Of course he can't play favorites, but I can tell he likes me.
Very GOOD!
Would you less talented students like to see WHAT NATE is doing?
He probably appreciAtes having a student like me who enjoys Art class and asks smart questions about art stuff.
NO, NATE... NO NUDE MODELS THIS YEAR...
DANG!
Peirce

THIS IS MY FAVORITE TIME OF THE SCHOOL YEAR! THE FIRST FEW WEEKS OF CLASSES!
LOOK AT ALL THOSE EAGER FACES! THEY LOOK SO ENTHUSIASTIC!
MOMENTS LIKE THIS GIVE ME HOPE FOR OUR YOUTH! THESE ARE GOOD KIDS! THEY WANT TO LEARN!
WHEN'S OUR FIRST FIELD TRIP?
Peirce

WHAT ARE YOU WORKING ON, NATE?
MY FIRST ART PROJECT OF THE YEAR, MR. ROSA!
GOOD GRAVY!
ISN'T IT COOL?
IT'S A BIT VIOLENT, ISN'T IT?
YOU CALL **THIS** VIOLENT? YOU HAVEN'T SEEN **ANYTHING** YET!
Peirce
SO MUCH FOR MY "HE'LL MATURE OVER THE SUMMER" THEORY....
HOW DO YOU DRAW A MACHINE GUN?

GIRLS!
Girls are kind of a pain, but it is sort of cool when you can tell they're looking at you and talking about you and stuff.
There's that guy NATE!
oooh!
At lunch all the cute girls sit at the same table. Francis and I sit in perfect position, only two tables away.
YAK! YAK! Chatter! Chatter!
voices of babes
It is like a challenge to try and get their attention. You have to know how to impress them, which I am pretty good at.
Look!
What's he doing?
HEY GIRLS! WATCH THIS! EIGHT FIG NEWTONS IN MY MOUTH AT ONCE!
I THINK I'LL MOVE TO THAT TABLE OVER THERE....
Peirce

EIGHT FIG NEWTONS IN MY MOUTH AT ONCE!
READY... GO!
NARF! NARF! NARF! NARF!
CHOMPF! CHOMPF! CHOMPF! CHOMPF!
THIS DOESN'T SEEM AS COOL AS IT DID A MINUTE AGO....
CHEW! CHEW!
Peirce

EIGHT FIG NEWTONS IN YOUR MOUTH AT ONCE! THIS MUST BE A WORLD RECORD!
MMPH! ORMF!
HI, FRANCIS.
HI.
HI, NATE.
ER... NATE CAN'T TALK. HE HAS LARYNGITIS.
LARYNGITIS? WHAT'S WITH HIS CHEEKS?
UH.... MUMPS! MUMPS, LARYNGITIS... HE'S A WALK-ING VIRUS FARM!
Peirce

THERE'S ONE SECOND LEFT IN THE GAME! NATE WRIGHT HAS THE BALL! HE SHOOTS!...
IT'S GOOD!
BUT WAIT! NOW FRANCIS GETS THE BALL! THERE'S STILL A TENTH OF A SECOND LEFT!
HE SHOOTS! YES!
BUT NOW NATE HAS THE BALL AGAIN! BY SOME MIRACLE THERE'S STILL A MILLIONTH OF A SECOND LEFT ON THE CLOCK!
IT'S UP! IT'S IN!
FRANCIS GETS THE BALL BACK! THERE'S STILL A QUADRILLIONTH OF A SECOND LEFT! HE SHOOTS!.... SWISH!
NATE GETS THE BALL ONE LAST TIME! THERE'S STILL A....A....
WHAT COMES AFTER A "QUADRILLIONTH"?
BEATS ME.
I QUIT! LET'S GO INSIDE!
I HATE SPORTS THAT REQUIRE MORE THAN A SIXTH-GRADE EDUCATION.

I'M THINKING OF RUNNING FOR CLASS PRESIDENT!
YOU?
6th GRADE CLASS ELECTION
SURE! I'D BE AN AWESOME PRESIDENT!
WHAT WOULD YOU ACCOMPLISH?
HUH?
I SAID, WHAT WOULD YOU ACCOMPLISH? WHY DO YOU WANT TO BE PRESIDENT?
I'D GET FREE ADMISSION TO ALL THE SCHOOL DANCES!
OH BROTHER...
Peirce

I'VE DECIDED TO RUN FOR CLASS PRESIDENT, FRANCIS! AND I WANT YOU TO BE MY CAMPAIGN MANAGER!
SORRY, I CAN'T.
WHY NOT?
BECAUSE I'M RUNNING FOR CLASS PRESIDENT MYSELF!
WHAT? YOU'D RUN AGAINST ME?
I HAPPEN TO THINK I'M THE BEST CANDIDATE FOR THE JOB.
Francis (EX-best friend)
Me
OW! Dog-gone it!
STAB STAB

CLASS ELECTIONS
I was all psyched about running for sixth-grade president, and then what happens? Francis decides HE'S going to run too!
"I happen to think I'm the best candidate for the job."
(his actual words)
F
He probably thinks he's going to win easy because he is such an egg-head. But am I going to give up? AS IF!!
I have an I.Q. of 158! YAK YAK drone drone...
I am going to campaign my head off. He won't know what hit him. I am going to beat him in this election no matter WHAT!!
NATE, I'D LIKE TO SPEAK TO YOU FOR A MOMENT.
FRANCIS: A STRONG LEADER (BUT SMELL ISN'T EVERYTHING!) VOTE NATE
Peirce

WHAT ARE YOU WORKING ON?
I GOT IN TROUBLE FOR MY FIRST BATCH OF CAMPAIGN POSTERS, SO I'M MAKING NEW ONES.
THEY SEEM A LITTLE BORING, THOUGH...
VOTE FOR NATE
THAT'S BECAUSE YOU'RE NOT TELLING THE VOTERS WHO YOU ARE! YOU NEED TO IDENTIFY YOURSELF!
WHAT DO YOU MEAN?
"VOTE FOR NATE: ELLEN'S BROTHER!"
HOO BOY...
Peirce

WHAT'S THAT?
NOT THAT IT'S ANY OF YOUR BEESWAX, BUT IT'S THE CAMPAIGN SPEECH I'M GIVING TO THE STUDENT BODY!
YEAH, I'VE GOT ONE TOO! I'VE BEEN WORKING ON IT ALL WEEK!
I'VE DEVELOPED A 10-POINT PLAN TO RADICALLY REVISE OUR STUDENT COUNCIL, RE-STRUCTURE THE 6TH GRADE SOCIAL EVENTS COMMITTEE, AND ESTABLISH A STUDENT JUDICIAL BOARD!
RIP!
Peirce

DID YOU FINISH COUNTING THE VOTES, MR. ROSA?
YUP! THE RESULTS ARE IN!
CLASS ELECTION TODAY
WELL, WHO WON? HIM OR ME?
NEITHER ONE OF YOU! THE WINNER WAS SHEILA STAPLETON!
WELL, I'M SURE **I** FINISHED A CLOSE SECOND!
I DIDN'T EVEN KNOW ANYBODY ELSE WAS **RUNNING!**
Peirce

BUT I DON'T **WANT** A HAIRCUT!
WELL, YOU'RE GETTING ONE.
I'M NOT LETTING THAT MOP GROW ANOTHER DAY!
HELP!
NATE, WILL YOU STOP MAKING SUCH A BIG DEAL OUT OF THIS?
WHEN I WAS YOUR AGE, I CUT MY **OWN** HAIR!
HOW COMFORTING.
STOP SQUIRMING, NATE! LIKE IT OR NOT, I AM **GOING** TO CUT YOUR HAIR!
... OR PERHAPS YOU'D RATHER MY LOVELY ASSISTANT TOOK OVER?
SNIP!
SNIP!
A LITTLE OFF THE TOP?
"LOVELY ASSISTANT"... VERY FUNNY.

I'M OFF TO SCHOOL! IS THIS MY LUNCH?
YUP.
WOW! COOKIES!
THEY'RE NOT COOKIES! THEY'RE OAT BRAN WAFERS!
THEY'RE LOW IN CHOLESTEROL! AND THEY'RE HIGH IN FIBER! THEY'RE GOOD FOR YOU! THEY'LL KEEP YOU REGULAR!
LIKE IT REALLY WOULD HAVE KILLED HIM TO LET ME GO ON THINKING THEY WERE COOKIES...
Peirce

HEY, MR. ROSA! LOOK WHAT I MADE!
SEE? WITH THIS PIECE OF CLAY, I MADE A LITTLE KITTY!
...AND WITH **THIS** PIECE OF CLAY, I MADE A HUGE STEAMROLLER!
GUESS WHAT'S GOING TO HAPPEN NEXT!
I COULDN'T POSSIBLY...
Peirce

HAVE YOU BOYS FINISHED YOUR CLAY SCULPTURES?
YUP! WE EACH MADE A LITTLE DOG! SEE?
BUT THESE ARE SO **TINY!** WHAT DID YOU DO WITH THE **REST** OF YOUR CLAY?
THE REST? UMMM.......
SMAK
I WIN! MINE'S STILL STUCK UP THERE!
DANG!
Peirce

HOMEWORK!
The school year has barely started, and already Mrs. Godfrey is going crazy with the home-work assignments.
Summer vacation is OVER, people! WA HA HA HA HAAAA!
What a sadist. Today she assigned us three chapters to read and a whole bunch of questions to answer.
THUD!
POINK!
So now I am sitting here at home and there is no way I am ever going to finish this stuff. In sit-uations like this there is only one thing to do.
HELLO, FRANCIS?
WHAT DO YOU WANT?
Peirce

FRANCIS, DID YOU DO THE SOCIAL STUDIES HOMEWORK?
YEAH, I DID IT.
WELL, GIVE ME THE ANSWERS! I CAN'T FIGURE THIS STUFF OUT!
I'M NOT GOING TO JUST **GIVE** YOU THE ANSWERS!
WHY NOT?
BECAUSE IT WOULD BE WRONG! YOU WON'T LEARN ANYTHING IF I DO ALL THE WORK **FOR** YOU!
I'VE GOT TO FIND A BEST FRIEND WITH A LESS RIGOROUS MORAL CODE....
Peirce

Detention!
Well, I got in trouble. Francis would not give me the answers for the Social Studies homework, so of course I had nothing to hand in.
PLEASE?!
No.
icicles
Naturally Godfrey threw a hairy and gave me detention. Right now I am sitting in the detention room. I have to sit here for a whole hour.
Detention Room
BOOT!
She told me to use the time to "think about what happened." She said there is a lesson to be learned from everything and that I am supposed to come to my own conclusion.
THIS IS ALL FRANCIS' FAULT.
Peirce

RAKE
RAKE
RAKE
RAKE
RAKE
RAKE
RAKE
RAKE
RAKE
RAKE
RAKE
HUFF! PUFF!
rake
rake
rake
GASP!
WHEW!
RAKE
RAKE
RAKE
I GUESS IT MUST BE FALL.
WHAT DO YOU MEAN?
DAD'S CHANGING COLOR.
GASP! PANT! WHEEZE!
Peirce

ARE YOU WATCHING THAT DUMB SOAP OPERA AGAIN?
IT'S NOT DUMB!
YES IT **IS**! IT'S SO BORING! **I** COULD WRITE A BETTER SOAP OPERA THAN THAT!
WELL, GO AHEAD AND DO IT, THEN!
YOU THINK I CAN'T?
I **KNOW** YOU CAN'T!
A NATE WRIGHT production
EVERLOVIN'
ELLEN!
The life and loves of a homely high school sophomore!
Hel-**LO**!
Take a hike!
Peirce

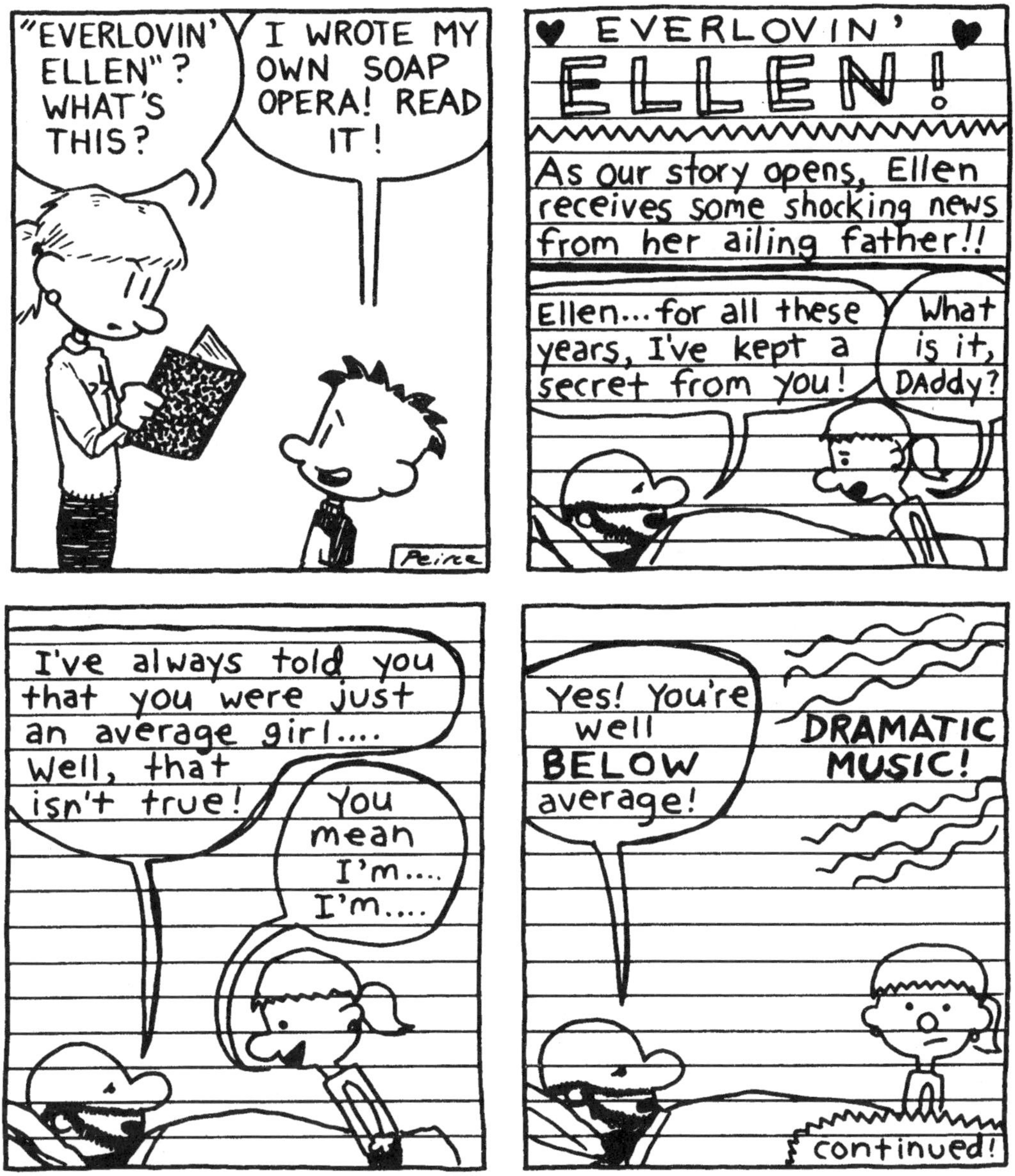
"EVERLOVIN' ELLEN"? WHAT'S THIS?
I WROTE MY OWN SOAP OPERA! READ IT!
Peirce
EVERLOVIN' ELLEN!
As our story opens, Ellen receives some shocking news from her ailing father!!
Ellen...for all these years, I've kept a secret from you!
What is it, DAddy?
I've always told you that you were just an average girl.... Well, that isn't true!
You mean I'm.... I'm....
Yes! You're well BELOW average!
DRAMATIC MUSIC!
continued!

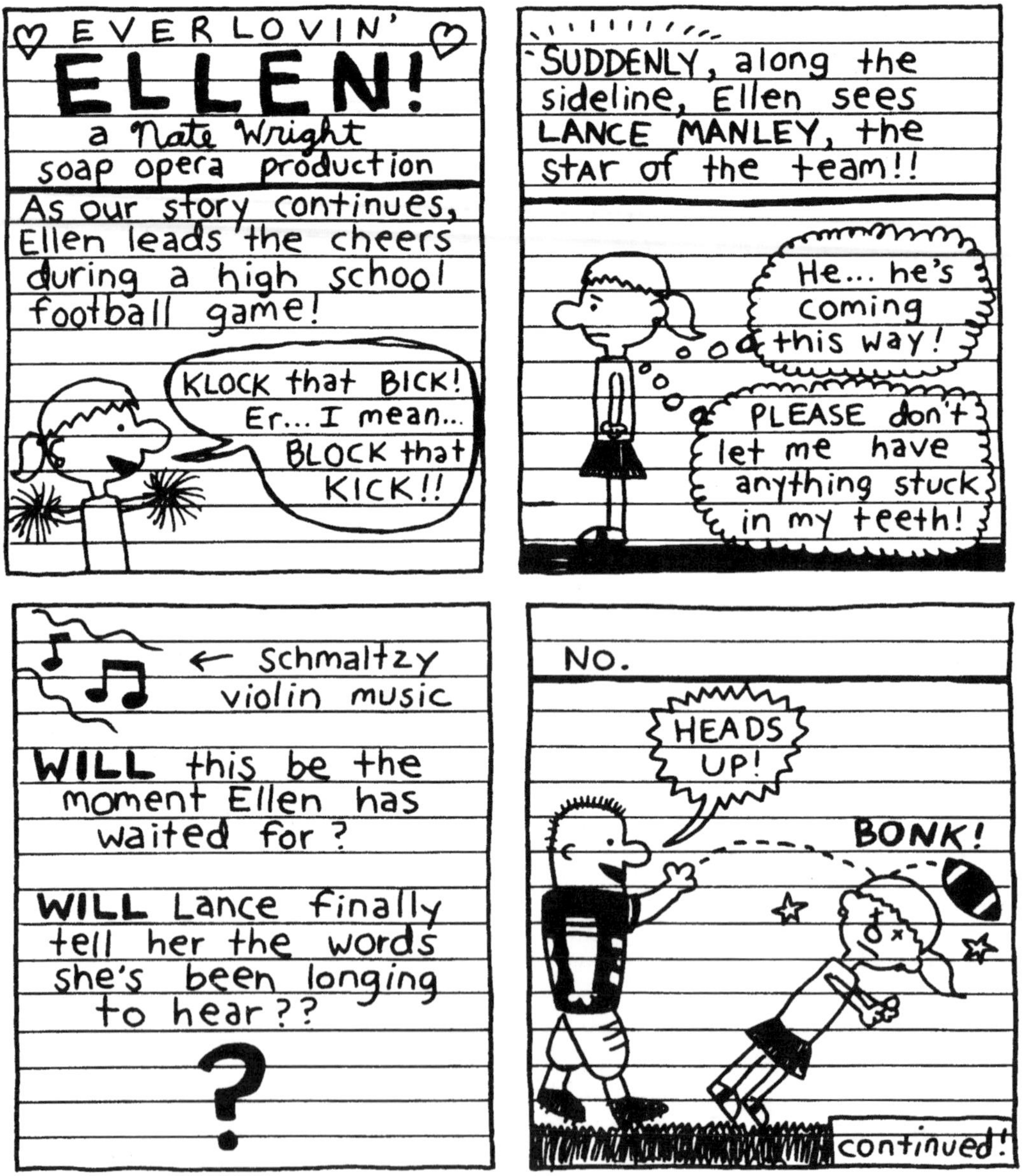
EVERLOVIN' ELLEN!
a Nate Wright soap opera production
As our story continues, Ellen leads the cheers during a high school football game!
KLOCK that BICK! Er... I mean... BLOCK that KICK!!
SUDDENLY, along the sideline, Ellen sees LANCE MANLEY, the star of the team!!
He... he's coming this way!
PLEASE don't let me have anything stuck in my teeth!
← Schmaltzy violin music
WILL this be the moment Ellen has waited for?
WILL Lance finally tell her the words she's been longing to hear??
?
No.
HEADS UP!
BONK!
continued!

WHEN YOU SAID YOU WERE GOING TO WRITE YOUR OWN SOAP OPERA, YOU DIDN'T SAY IT WOULD BE ABOUT ME!
NO NEED TO THANK ME!
Peirce
Knocked unconscious by a football, Ellen wakes up in a hospital bed!
Where am I?
In the hospital! That was quite a nasty concussion you had!
DR. Cesspool →
Am I going to be all right, Doctor?
Sure! You're going to be just fine!
What a RELIEF!
But while you're here, can I interest you in a nose job?
continued!

EVERLOVIN'
ELLEN!
(a Nate Wright production)
Ellen is visited in the hospital by LANCE, the captain of the football team!
♥ LANCE! ♥
Hi
Ellen... something wonderful has happened while you've been unconscious!
Yes, Lance?
As I sat by your bedside, waiting for you to wake up.... I discovered TRUE LOVE!
You mean....?
Yup! I'm eloping with one of the nurses!
C'mon, lamb-chop!

SO WHAT DID YOU THINK OF THE SOAP OPERA I WROTE?
WHAT DID I THINK OF IT?
RIP! RIP!
RIP
RIP
RIP
STOMP!
STOM
STOM
STOM
STOM
ANOTHER SUCCESS!

GO OUT, FRANCIS! GO WAY OUT!
WHY ARE YOU STOPPING? GO LONG! I'M GONNA THROW A BOMB!
I DON'T THINK YOU CAN THROW IT ANY FARTHER THAN THIS.
WHAT? SURE I CAN! KEEP RUNNING!
I'LL STAY RIGHT HERE, THANKS.
FINE! BUT WHEN THE BALL FLIES OVER YOUR HEAD AND YOU HAVE TO CHASE IT, DON'T COME CRYING TO ME!
HEAVE!
TRICKLE!
BOUNCE!
BOUNCE!
HERE. YOU DROPPED THIS.
HA HA. THE WIND WAS AGAINST ME, THAT'S ALL!

THE BELL'S ABOUT TO RING, AND NATE ISN'T HERE!
COULD IT BE? MAYBE HE'S ABSENT! WHAT A RELIEF! A ONE-DAY REPRIEVE FROM NATE!
RRRIINNG!
HEL-**LO**!
I LIKE TO RAISE HER HOPES, THEN DASH THEM TO PIECES!
PEIRCE

RUSTLE!
CRUMPLE!
SHRED!
SHUFFLE!
BOY, ARE YOU EVER A SLOB!
I DON'T LIKE THE WORD "SLOB!"
OH?
I PREFER TO THINK OF MYSELF AS "ORGANIZATIONALLY CHALLENGED!"
Peirce

MAN! LOOK AT ALL THAT JUNK IN YOUR NOTEBOOK! WHAT DO YOU USE ALL THAT PAPER FOR?
YANK!
CRUMPLE! CRUMPLE!
AMMO!
OOOH! GODFREY'S BACK IS TURNED! AIM FOR HER HEAD!
Peirce

NATE, YOU HAVE THE MESSIEST NOTEBOOK I'VE EVER SEEN!
I'VE SEEN **PIG-STIES** THAT LOOKED NEATER!
I'LL BET YOU HAVE.
Peirce
PEN SWEET PEN
Th-th-th-THAT'S ALL, FOLKS!
Oink!
Honey, I'm HOME!

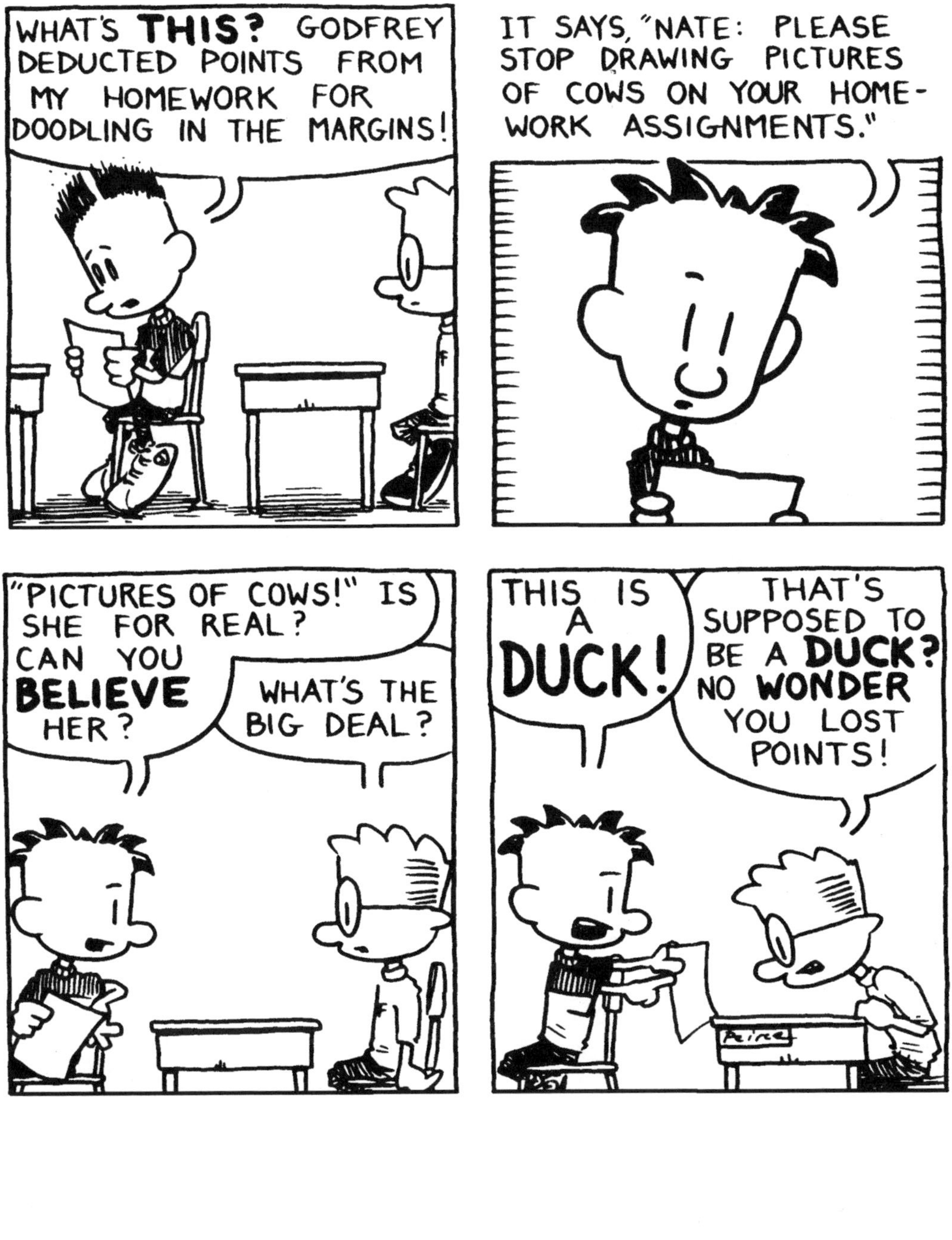
WHAT'S THIS? GODFREY DEDUCTED POINTS FROM MY HOMEWORK FOR DOODLING IN THE MARGINS!
IT SAYS, "NATE: PLEASE STOP DRAWING PICTURES OF COWS ON YOUR HOME-WORK ASSIGNMENTS."
"PICTURES OF COWS!" IS SHE FOR REAL? CAN YOU BELIEVE HER?
WHAT'S THE BIG DEAL?
THIS IS A DUCK!
THAT'S SUPPOSED TO BE A DUCK? NO WONDER YOU LOST POINTS!

LISTEN TO THIS NOTE FROM GODFREY!..."NATE: IF YOU CONTINUE TO PASS IN HOMEWORK THAT IS MESSY AND CRUMPLED, I WILL DEDUCT POINTS FROM YOUR SCORE!"
CAN YOU BELIEVE HER? LOWERING MY SCORE BECAUSE MY WORK ISN'T NEAT ENOUGH?!
WHAT AN OUTRAGE! NEATNESS HAS NOTHING TO DO WITH QUALITY!
MY WORK IS MEDIOCRE WHETHER IT'S NEAT OR NOT!
THAT'S THE SPIRIT.
PEIRCE

He's BACK! The world's only bald super-hero!
SWOOP!
IT'S.... SUPERDAD!!
It's a typical Sunday morning, and SUPERDAD is demonstrating his ultra-wicked powers!
OOF!
Darn this Sunday paper!
HE LIFTS HEAVY OBJECTS!
These socks have HAD it!
HE DISPOSES OF TOXIC WASTES!!
Who wants marmalade?
MARMALADE, anyone?
AND HE STILL FINDS TIME TO FIX BREAKFAST!
DANG!
What's wrong with this jar?
Grunt!
It won't open!
Allow ME!
TWIST!
THERE YOU GO!
WELL, SURE, AFTER I LOOSENED IT UP FOR YOU!
Peirce

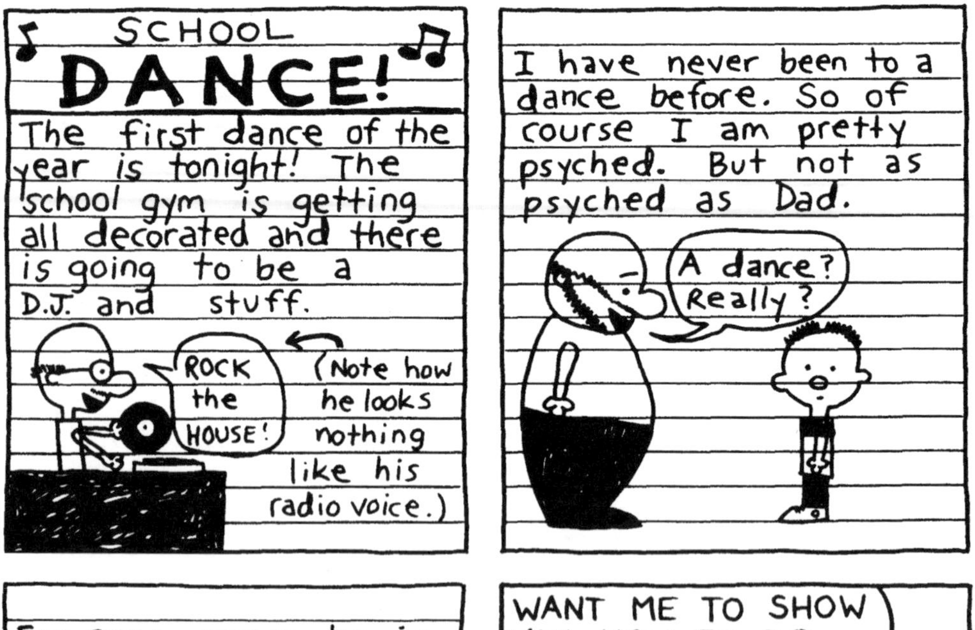
SCHOOL DANCE!
The first dance of the year is tonight! The school gym is getting all decorated and there is going to be a D.J. and stuff.
ROCK the HOUSE!
(Note how he looks nothing like his radio voice.)
I have never been to a dance before. So of course I am pretty psyched. But not as psyched as Dad.
A dance? Really?
For some reason he is really into this being my first dance. I don't know what the big deal is, but he is totally out of control.
You know, I used to be quite a dancer myself!
WANT ME TO SHOW YOU HOW TO DO "THE HUSTLE"?
GET REAL, DAD.
Peirce

WOW! OUR FIRST DANCE!
I KNOW! THIS IS **WICKED!**
DA
AS SOON AS WE WALK OUT ON THAT DANCE FLOOR, WE'RE NOT KIDS ANYMORE!
YOU SAID IT!
THIS IS THE NIGHT WE BECOME **MEN!**
RIGHT!
YOU FIRST.
NO, **YOU** FIRST!
PEIRCE

AT THE
Dance!
It is kind of weird being at a dance and seeing all the girls that you see in school every day. At a dance they act kind of different.
(they travel in packs)
They stand around and wait for YOU to ask them to dance. So it's like: the pressure is ON!
girls
(opposite ends of the floor.)
guys
But it is important not to rush into anything. You have to be cool and take your time. Fortunately, being cool is my specialty.
WE'VE BEEN SITTING HERE FOR TWO HOURS. MAYBE WE SHOULD MAKE OUR MOVE.
UH..... I DON'T LIKE THIS SONG! LET'S WAIT FOR A GOOD SONG!

MR. ROSA! WHAT ARE **YOU** DOING HERE?
I'M ONE OF THE FACULTY CHAPERONES!
WHY AREN'T YOU DANCING, NATE? FIND YOURSELF A PARTNER AND HIT THAT DANCE FLOOR!
I WILL IF YOU WILL.
WHO, **ME?** WELL...... I..... UH....
THERE'S MISS BURTON, THE SCHOOL NURSE! HOW'D YOU LIKE TO GET A CHECK-UP FROM **HER**?
Peirce

COME ON, NATE! GET WITH THE PROGRAM!
WHY DON'T YOU DANCE?
I DON'T WANT TO LOOK STUPID.
YOU MEAN, STUPIDER THAN YOU LOOK SITTING HERE ALL BY YOURSELF?
GOOD POINT.
Peirce

GO ON AND ASK SOMEONE TO DANCE, NATE! YOU CAN DO IT!
WELL... OKAY.
MR. ROSA! SHE SAID YES!
WHO SAID YES?
THAT'S FUNNY. SHE WAS RIGHT BEHIND ME.
PEIRCE

WHEW! THAT WAS GREAT!
I'M A DANCIN' FOOL, IF I DO SAY SO MYSELF!
HOW MANY TIMES DID YOU DANCE?
I LOST COUNT! BUT I DANCED THREE TIMES WITH JENNY!
YOU DID? SHE IS SUCH A BABE!
I KNOW! AND SHE'S AN AWESOME DANCER!
DID YOU SEE EDDIE BURKE TRYING TO DANCE?
HEE HEE! YEAH! WHAT A STIFF! AND HE EVEN DANCED A SLOW ONE WITH NINA MCFADDEN!
HE DID? I CAN'T BELIEVE I MISSED THAT!
I THINK YOU WERE DANCING WITH MARY AT THE TIME!
MAN! WHAT A NIGHT!
THAT WAS THE MOST FUN I'VE EVER HAD IN MY LIFE!
WRIGHT
HI, NATE! HOW WAS THE DANCE?
IT WAS OKAY.
Peirce

I'M WORKING FOR THE SCHOOL NEWSPAPER AGAIN THIS YEAR, FRANCIS!
WHEREVER THERE'S NEWS, THAT'S WHERE I'LL BE! I'LL BE FERRETING OUT CORRUPTION AND UN-COVERING SCANDALS!
YUP! THEY DON'T CALL ME "SCOOP" FOR NOTHING!
THEY DON'T CALL YOU "SCOOP" AT ALL!
YOU'RE JUST JEALOUS THAT YOU DON'T HAVE A COOL NICKNAME!
Peirce

SO, "SCOOP," WHAT'S YOUR NEXT ARTICLE GOING TO BE ABOUT?
I WAS JUST TRYING TO FIGURE THAT OUT MYSELF...
I'VE GOT IT! I'LL DO A STORY ABOUT YOU!
ME?
IT'LL BE A STORY ABOUT BEING A NERDY TEACHER'S PET! I'LL CALL IT "FRANCIS: PORTRAIT OF A GEEK!"
IT'LL BE A HARD-HITTING EXPOSÉ!
HARDER-HITTING THAN YOU THINK.
Peirce

HOW GOES IT, "SCOOP"?
I'VE LOOKED ALL OVER THIS DUMB SCHOOL, AND I CAN'T UNCOVER ANY JUICY SCANDALS!
HOW AM I SUPPOSED TO BE AN ACE REPORTER WHEN THERE'S NOTHING GOING ON? I NEED TO FIND A SMOKING GUN!
SWEEP! SWEEP!
HOW ABOUT A SMOKING JANITOR?
GAD, THIS PLACE IS BORING!

Rusty Sienna is back on t.v. for another season of "Oil Painting With Rusty," and guess what? Dad bought me my own paint set!
GA-BOING!
PAINT
Of course I have always been Rusty's #1 fan, but now I will finally be more than just a spectator.
Let's paint, dag-nab it!
Now I can paint along with Rusty. Of all the presents Dad has ever given me, this is the greatest. My own paint set!
OOPS.
WHAT HAVE I DONE?
PEIRCE

NOW, FRIENDS, AS YOU CAN SEE, I'M OPENING UP MY TUBE OF "SAP GREEN."
NOW I'M GOING TO APPLY THE PAINT IN A SERIES OF QUICK, VIGOROUS STROKES!
BRUSHA! BRUSHA! BRUSHA!
THERE! WE MADE A TREE! YOU'RE DOING GREAT!

OKAY, NOW LET'S PAINT A LITTLE CABIN....
BRUSH! BRUSH! BRUSH!
... AND NEXT TO THE CABIN ARE SOME LITTLE TREES PROVIDING SHADE...
BRUSH! BRUSH! BRUSH!
... AND STANDING IN THE SHADE IS A LITTLE DEER....
BRUSH! BRUSH! BRUSH!
WAIT UP!
... AND NEXT TO THE DEER IS A TINY LEPRECHAUN...
PEIRCE

SNAP!
GRIND
GRIND
GRIND
GRIND
GRIND
GRIND
GRIND
GRIND
GRIND
GRIND
GRIND GRIND
GRIND
GRIND
GRIND
SNAP!
Peirce

'BYE, ELLEN. SEE YOU TOMORROW.
'BYE, CAROL.
OMIGOSH! IT'S KENNY SMITHSON, THE CAPTAIN OF THE FOOTBALL TEAM! WHAT A HUNK! AND HE'S COMING THIS WAY!
IS HE LOOKING AT ME? I THINK HE'S LOOKING AT ME! HE **IS** LOOKING AT ME! WHY IS HE LOOKING AT ME?
THERE'S SOMETHING HANGING FROM MY NOSE.... I **KNOW** IT!
HI.

I DON'T BELIEVE IT! I'M STANDING HERE HAVING A CONVERSATION WITH KENNY SMITHSON!
I DIDN'T THINK HE EVEN KNEW MY NAME! AND HE CAME RIGHT UP AND STARTED TALKING WITH ME!
I GUESS IT'S TRUE WHAT THEY SAY: JUST WHEN YOU LEAST EXPECT IT, SOMEONE CAN WALK INTO YOUR LIFE!
HEL-LO!
OH NO.....

BEAT IT, NATE! CAN'T YOU SEE I'M HAVING A PRIVATE CONVERSATION?
OKAY! FINE! I CAN TAKE A HINT! I KNOW WHEN I'M NOT WANTED!
YOU TWO KIDS JUST CONTINUE WHAT YOU WERE DOING! I'LL GO SIT QUIETLY OVER HERE! YOU WON'T EVEN KNOW I'M AROUND!
High School
CONFIDENTIAL!
(This ACTUALLY happened!)
Hey babe! Wanna play "tonsil hockey?"
Ellen
Some guy

High School
CONFIDENTIAL!
ACTUAL EVENTS!
ACTUAL DIALOGUE!
It's so COOL that you're captain of the football team, Kenny!
Thanks!
I've noticed you on the sidelines during games! I think you're the best cheerleader!
You DO?
pound! pound!
Ellen... there's something I've GOT to ask you!
Yes, Kenny?
flutter! flutter!
WHO'S THE KID WITH THE NOTEBOOK?
LOUDER! SPEAK UP, YOU TWO!
Peirce

LISTEN, I'D BETTER GO! I'M GONNA BE LATE FOR PRACTICE!
OKAY.
BUT... UM... WELL... WOULD YOU LIKE TO GO TO A MOVIE OR SOMETHING WITH ME SOMETIME?
SURE!
GREAT! 'BYE!
SMAK!
I.... I'LL NEVER WASH MY LIPS AGAIN!
DID YOU EVER?
Peirce

HE KISSED ME! KENNY SMITHSON ACTUALLY KISSED ME!
HE JUST LEANED OVER, AND HE KISSED ME!
IF ONLY THERE WERE A WAY OF PRESERVING THAT MOMENT FOREVER!
Kiss me, you fool!
BONK!
OW! DAG!
Peirce

HAVE YOU GOT YOUR ORAL REPORT READY FOR SOCIAL STUDIES?
NOPE!
YOU DON'T? BUT IT'S DUE TODAY!
NOT FOR ME! MRS. GODFREY ALWAYS HAS US DO OUR REPORTS IN ALPHABETICAL ORDER!
MY NAME'S "WRIGHT!" I'M A "W!" SHE WON'T GET TO ME UNTIL TOMORROW!
YOU ALWAYS DO THIS! YOU DON'T DO YOUR WORK, AND THEN WHEN YOU GET IN TROUBLE, YOU FIND A WAY TO BLAME SOMEBODY ELSE!
ME?? I DO NOT!
YES YOU DO! YOU'VE ALWAYS GOT AN EXCUSE! IT'S ALWAYS ANYONE'S FAULT BUT YOUR OWN!
YOU'RE NUTS, FRANCIS! YOU DON'T KNOW WHAT YOU'RE TALKING ABOUT!
RRING!
CLASS, I'VE DECIDED THAT THIS WEEK, WE'LL GIVE OUR REPORTS STARTING AT THE END OF THE ALPHABET!
THAT'S YOU, NATE!
LEAVE IT TO WENDY ZIMMERMAN TO BE ABSENT TODAY.
Peirce

LOOK, DAD! I FOUND A BOOK ON CHINESE ASTROLOGY!
IT'S WICKED! YOU CAN FIND OUT ALL SORTS OF STUFF ABOUT SOMEBODY JUST FROM WHEN THEY WERE BORN!
YOU, FOR EXAMPLE, WERE BORN IN THE "YEAR OF THE PIG"!
I'LL REFRAIN FROM MAKING THE OBVIOUS JOCULAR COMMENT!
I APPRECIATE THAT.
Peirce

I'VE BEEN DOING SOME MORE READING IN MY ASTROLOGY BOOK, DAD!
HERE'S WHAT IT SAYS ABOUT **YOU!**.... "YOURS IS A COMMANDING PRESENCE! YOUR PHYSICAL MAGNETISM AND SENSE OF SELF ENSURE THAT HEADS WILL TURN WHEN YOU ENTER A ROOM!"
"THE PICTURE OF SELF-CONFIDENCE, YOU EFFORTLESSLY EARN THE....(HEE HEE!).... RESPECT AND EVEN...(SNICKER!)... **AWE** OF YOUR PEERS!"
OH HO HO HO HO! HA HA!
THIS IS ONE OF THE MOST HILARIOUS BOOKS I'VE EVER READ!
Peirce

DAD, CAN WE GET A DOG?
NATE, WE'VE HAD THIS TALK A THOUSAND TIMES! AND YOU KNOW HOW I FEEL!
I'M NOT GOING TO SPEND MY HARD-EARNED MONEY ON SOMETHING THAT DOES NOTHING BUT EAT, SLEEP, AND MAKE NOISE!
BUT....
WATCH IT.
PEIRCE

COME ON, NATE! I WANT YOU TO HELP ME CLEAN OUT THE GARAGE!
THIS WILL BE FUN! WE CAN TALK WHILE WE WORK! IT'LL HELP PASS THE TIME!
A FATHER AND HIS SON SHOULD DO THINGS LIKE THIS TOGETHER! THIS IS ONE OF THOSE "BONDING" EXPERIENCES THAT ARE SO IMPORTANT!
WHY DO THESE "BONDING" EXPERIENCES ALWAYS IN-VOLVE MANUAL LABOR?
Peirce

BILLS, BILLS, BILLS! HOW AM I GOING TO PAY ALL THESE?
THIS IS RIDICULOUS! THE BILLS NEVER STOP! DO THESE PEOPLE THINK I'M MADE OF MONEY?
SAY, DAD, SPEAKING OF MONEY.... HOW ABOUT A RAISE IN MY ALLOWANCE?
I HAVE GOT TO WORK ON MY TIMING.
Peirce

HEY DAD! WHAT DID THE DALAI LAMA SAY TO THE HOT DOG VENDOR?
"MAKE ME ONE WITH EVERYTHING!"
OH HO HO HO HO HO WA HA HA HA HA HA
IT MUST BE NICE TO BE YOUR OWN BEST AUDIENCE.
HERE'S ANOTHER ONE! A CAMEL AND A DUCK ARE WALKING DOWN THE STREET!....
Peirce

HI, THERE! AND WELCOME TO "OIL PAINTING WITH RUSTY!"
I'M YOUR HOST, RUSTY SIENNA!
WELL, FRIENDS, WHAT SHALL WE PAINT TODAY?
A WOMAN.
A WOMAN OF UNCOMMON BEAUTY! A WOMAN WITH SILKEN BLOND HAIR! A WOMAN WITH IVORY WHITE TEETH!
A CARING WOMAN! AN UNDERSTANDING WOMAN! A WOMAN UNAFRAID TO SPEAK HER MIND AND FOLLOW HER HEART!
A WOMAN WITH PIERCING BLUE EYES WHICH GAZE STRAIGHT INTO THE DEPTHS OF MY VERY SOUL!!
A MOUNTAIN? GOOD!
NUTS.
DO YOU MIND?

STANDARDIZED
TEST!
A few weeks ago in school we took what is called a "vocational aptitude" test. Today we are getting the results.
Okay, people, break out those #2 pencils!
NO, you can't use a PEN! Did you hear me say "pen"?
The way the test works is: You answer all sorts of "multiple-choice" questions about your abilities and interests and stuff.
DANG these little ovals!
Then a computer analyzes the answers you gave and tells you what kind of a career you are going to have.
SOMETHING LUCRATIVE, I HOPE.
TELL ME ABOUT IT! MY ALLOWANCE IS PATHETIC!
Peirce

MY STANDARDIZED TEST RESULTS SAY I'M GOOD AT "ANALYTICAL THINKING."
OOOOOH! NOW FOR MY RESULTS!
"YOU ARE A GENIUS."
WHAT IS THIS, SOME SORT OF CANDID CAMERA THING?
YES!
Peirce

YOUR STANDARDIZED TEST RESULTS SAY YOU'RE A **GENIUS?**
IT'S A DIRTY JOB, BUT **SOMEONE'S** GOT TO DO IT!
IT **IS** KIND OF A BIG RESPONSIBILITY! THINK OF ALL THE GOOD YOU COULD DO! THE GREAT DEEDS YOU COULD ACCOMPLISH!
SO WHAT ARE YOU GOING TO DO FIRST?
QUIT SCHOOL, OF COURSE!
OF COURSE.
IF **YOU** WERE A GENIUS, FRANCIS, YOU WOULDN'T HAVE EVEN **ASKED** THAT QUESTION!
Peirce

I STILL CAN'T BELIEVE YOUR TEST RESULTS SAY YOU'RE A GENIUS.
BELIEVE IT, FRANCIS! IT'S RIGHT HERE IN BLACK AND WHITE!
NATE? HI. I THINK THERE WAS SOME SORT OF MIX-UP.
I GOT YOUR TEST RESULTS AND YOU GOT MINE. HERE.
WHAT'S THE GOOD WORD, EINSTEIN?
I CAN'T LOOK...
PEIRCE

LOOK, ELLEN! THE LATEST EDITION OF "DR. CESSPOOL COMICS"!
GREAT.
DR. CESSPOOL and his faithful nurse, MAUREEN BIOLOGY, are re-attaching the head of the famous race car driver JEAN-CLAUDE CLOD, decapitated in a crash!
Doctor! You've re-attached his head BACKWARDS!
I have? Whoopsy!
Well... so his head is on backwards! Let's look on the bright side!
The BRIGHT side?
This could COMPLETELY eliminate the need for rear-view mirrors!

REMEMBER WHEN YOU SAID MY "DOCTOR CESSPOOL COMICS" DIDN'T HAVE ENOUGH RO-MANCE IN THEM? WELL, CHECK THIS OUT!
Dr. Cesspool and his faithful nurse, MAUREEN BIOLOGY, share a tender moment!
Sniff! Sniff! SAY! What's that BEWITCH-ING scent?
Formaldehyde! I wore it just for you!
Oh Nurse!
Oh Doctor!
SMAK!
HOW TORRID CAN YOU GET?
CAREFUL YOU DON'T BURN YOUR HANDS!
Peirce

HERE'S THE SANDWICH YOU ASKED FOR.
ABOUT TIME, NATE! I SENT YOU OFF TO MAKE THIS TEN MINUTES AGO!
SNATCH!
HEY! WHAT HAPPENED TO THIS SANDWICH?
WHAT DO YOU MEAN?
LOOK AT IT! IT'S ALL HACKED UP! IT'S TOTALLY MANGLED!
WELL? WHAT'S THE DEAL, NATE? WHY DOES THIS THING LOOK LIKE SOMEBODY USED IT AS A HOCKEY PUCK?
DID YOU OR DID YOU NOT TELL ME TO GET YOU A TUNA SANDWICH "AND STEP ON IT"?
OH, GROSS...
I KNEW I'D FIND A USE FOR DAD'S GOLF SHOES ONE OF THESE DAYS!
Peirce

THAT MRS. GODFREY IS THE **WORST**!
SLAM!
WHAT DID SHE DO?
SHE KEEPS ASKING ME QUESTIONS IN CLASS! SHE CALLS ON ME AT LEAST ONCE A DAY! AND I DON'T EVEN RAISE MY HAND!
SHE **KNOWS** I WON'T GET IT RIGHT, BUT SHE GOES AHEAD AND ASKS **ANYWAY**! EVERY DAY, LIKE CLOCKWORK!
THE NERVE OF SOME PEOPLE.
I'LL SAY! CAN'T THIS WOMAN TAKE "I DON'T KNOW" FOR AN ANSWER?

The Adventures Of TEDDY the TURKEY!
Gobble gobble gobble
Gobble Gobble Gobble
2 Days later:
Gobble Gobble Gobble
Teddy
Gobble Gobble Gobble
TEDDY'S ADVENTURES ARE SOMEWHAT ABBREVIATED.
I KNOW! I ONLY HAD ONE SHEET OF PAPER!
Peirce

THANKSGIVING AT ENGINE COMPANY #25!
Happy Thanksgiving, fellers!
Happy Thanks...
RING!
E-GAD! A fire!
A BIG one! I can see the smoke!
Let's go!
Oh NO! Not THIS house again!
Every Thanksgiving it's the same thing!
THE MEAT MAY BE A LITTLE TOUGH....
I'LL CALL "PIZZA HUT."
Peirce

AAAH! THANKSGIVING DINNER! THIS LOOKS DELICIOUS, IF I DO SAY SO MYSELF!
NATE? WOULD YOU LIKE TO SAY GRACE?
MMPHGRF!
NATE?
GRMPH! CHOMPF! CHOMPF!
ANOTHER FAMILY MOMENT TO CHERISH...
SMACK! SMACK! IS THERE GRAVY? SEND THAT GRAVY DOWN HERE!
Peirce

WELL, WE'VE EATEN OUR FILL OF TURKEY WITH ALL THE TRIMMINGS... WE'VE HAD DESSERT....
WE'VE CLEARED THE TABLE... DONE THE DISHES.... PUT AWAY THE LEFTOVERS....
NOTHING LEFT TO DO BUT GATHER IN THE LIVING ROOM AND EXCHANGE THANKSGIVING GIFTS!
LET'S START WITH YOU, DAD! WHAT DID YOU GET ME?

It's the annual Wright family Thanksgiving football game!
And DAD fields the kick-off!
voices of play-by-play men.
He heads upfield! He's at the 30!... The 40!...
He's at the 50!.... The 40!... The 30!...
He's at the 20!... He's.... He's...
WAIT a minute! He's slowing down!
GASP! I'M GOING IN!
ALREADY? WE JUST GOT OUT HERE!
N
Peirce

WHO DO YOU THINK IS THE CUTEST GIRL IN SCHOOL?
THAT'S EASY! JENNY!
SHE IS QUITE THE BABE....
UNFORTUNATELY, I NEVER HAVE A CHANCE TO TALK TO HER!
SEE? SHE'S SO POPULAR, SHE'S ALWAYS SURROUNDED BY A MOB OF PEOPLE!
I'D GIVE ANYTHING IF JUST ONCE I HAD THE CHANCE TO TALK TO HER ALONE!
ANYTHING?
ANYTHING!
EVEN YOUR BANANA?
MY BANANA? WHAT DOES THAT HAVE TO..... ?
HEY, JENNY! COME HERE! NATE WANTS TO TALK TO YOU!! ALONE!
MMMMMM! NO BRUISES!
NOT YET.
Peirce

GODFREY POSTED THE PAIRINGS FOR THE NEXT PROJECT.
AND LOOK! YOU AND I ARE ASSIGNED TO WORK TOGETHER!
WE'RE PARTNERS! AND YOU'RE ONE OF THE BIGGEST BRAINS IN SCHOOL! WHAT LUCK!
I'M PRACTICALLY GUARANTEED A GOOD GRADE! WHY, THIS COULD BE THE FIRST "A" OF MY CAREER!
...OR THE FIRST "D" OF MINE.
Peirce

OKAY, OUR REPORT TOPIC IS "LOUISIANA."
OOOOOOH! "LAISSEZ LES BON TEMPS ROULLER!"
WE'VE GOT A FREE PERIOD! LET'S HIT THE LIBRARY!
THE LIBRARY?
OF COURSE! WE HAVE TO DO RESEARCH!
RESEARCH?
YES! DO YOU THINK THIS REPORT IS GOING TO WRITE ITSELF?
NO, I FIGURED YOU'D WRITE IT! I'LL HANDLE THE ILLUS-TRATIONS!
Peirce

OKAY, I'VE COMPILED ALL THE SIGNIFICANT HISTORICAL EVENTS FOR OUR REPORT ON LOUISIANA... I'VE ARRANGED THEM IN CHRONOLOGICAL ORDER.... AND I'VE WRITTEN BRIEF PROFILES OF ALL THE IMPORTANT SOCIAL AND POLITICAL FIGURES IN THE STATE'S HISTORY.
WHAT HAVE **YOU** DONE?
I'VE DRAWN A PICTURE OF A PELICAN!
WHY?
WHY? BECAUSE IT'S THE OFFICIAL STATE BIRD! COME **ON**, FRANCIS! DO I HAVE TO DO **ALL** THE WORK AROUND HERE?
Peirce

OKAY, THE "LOUISIANA PURCHASE" TOOK PLACE IN 1803....
I THINK IT'S COOL THAT THE STATE BIRD OF LOUISIANA IS THE PELICAN!
...LOUISIANA WAS ADMITTED TO STATEHOOD IN 1812....
CHECK OUT THIS DRAWING, FRANCIS! SEE? IT'S A PELICAN!
...THE BATTLE OF NEW ORLEANS WAS FOUGHT IN 1815....
I WONDER IF DAD WOULD LET ME HAVE A PELICAN FOR A PET.... PROBABLY NOT.
WILL YOU **FORGET** THE STUPID PELICAN ALREADY??
I MEAN, THE MAN WON'T EVEN LET ME HAVE A **GERBIL**!
Peirce

OKAY, I'VE FINISHED MY PART OF OUR REPORT ON LOUISIANA.
ME TOO!
HERE'S MY HALF. I DID FIVE PAGES.
HERE'S MINE! I DID **TEN!**
THESE ARE ALL DRAWINGS OF PELICANS.
EXACTLY! THE STATE BIRD OF LOUISIANA!
I THINK **MY** NAME SHOULD COME FIRST ON THE COVER, FRANCIS! I DID **TWICE** AS MANY PAGES AS YOU DID!
Peirce

WHAT ARE **YOU** SO MAD ABOUT?
WHAT DO YOU **THINK**, NATE? I ENDED UP DOING ALL THE WORK FOR OUR SOCIAL STUDIES REPORT!
WHAT?? WHAT ABOUT ALL THOSE DRAWINGS I MADE?
BIG DEAL! WHO DID ALL THE RESEARCH? WHO DID ALL THE WRITING? **ME!**
WE WERE SUPPOSED TO BE **PARTNERS**, NATE! PARTNERS ARE SUPPOSED TO **SHARE!**
SPEAKING OF SHARING... ARE YOU GOING TO FINISH THAT TWINKIE?
YES!
Peirce

NATE, COME UP TO THE BLACKBOARD, PLEASE.
OH, MAN!...
WRITE THE NAMES OF THE NEW ENGLAND STATES AND THEIR CAPITALS.
OH NO! I DON'T KNOW THIS STUFF!
WHY DOES GODFREY ALWAYS PICK ON ME? THE WOMAN HATES ME! SHE TOTALLY HATES ME!
WHAT AM I GONNA DO? I DON'T KNOW THE ANSWERS! I CAN'T JUST GUESS! BUT WHAT ELSE CAN I DO?
I CAN'T JUST STAND HERE LIKE AN IDIOT! I GOTTA GET OUT OF THIS! I'VE GOT TO DO SOMETHING! ANYTHING! I'VE GOT TO.....
SCREEE
DETENTION
I'M A VICTIM OF MY OWN INGENUITY.
Peirce

Mr. ROSA!
Mr. Rosa is one of those teachers that, no matter when you go into his class-room, he is there.
Hey HEY HEY!
Sometimes if you go into his room after school, he is in there working on one of his own paintings. And if you are quiet, he will let you sit and watch.
DANG, I'm good!
That is what happened today. I was watching Mr. ROSA paint and then suddenly a question popped into my mind:
THIS GUY IS OUR ART TEACHER?
WHAT DO YOU THINK?
Peirce

WHAT DO YOU THINK OF MY LATEST PAINTING, NATE?
I DON'T GET IT.
WELL, IT'S AN ABSTRACTION! IT'S PURELY AN EXERCISE IN COLOR AND FORM!
YEAH, BUT.... HOW DO YOU KNOW... I MEAN.... HOW CAN YOU TELL....?
....WHAT IT MEANS?
NO, WHETHER YOU HAVE ANY ACTUAL TALENT.
Peirce

THIS "ABSTRACT" STUFF IS OKAY, MR. ROSA, BUT CAN'T YOU DO ANY **REAL** ART?
SURE!
WHAT WOULD YOU LIKE ME TO DRAW?
A DOG!
THERE!
SAAAY! MR. ROSA! THAT'S NOT **BAD**!
OF COURSE, YOU'RE NO RUSTY SIENNA!
WELL, IT'S SOMETHING TO AIM FOR...
Peirce

CHRISTMAS
is less than 2 weeks away!
HO HO HO!
AWESOME! Christmas is my favorite holiday.
The best part about Christmas is all the presents. I am trying to figure out what Dad got me, but he is being wicked sneaky. He has done a good job of hiding stuff.
Tippy-toe Tippy-toe
But I am not giving up. Somewhere in this house he is hiding my Christmas presents, and I am going to keep looking until I find them.
? ?
JUST BROWSING?
ER.... HI, DAD.
peirce

I'VE WRITTEN A CHRISTMAS LIST, DAD, IN CASE YOU'RE HAVING TROUBLE BUYING ME PRESENTS!
HOW THOUGHT-FUL.
NUMBER ONE: A DOG!
HOLD IT! YOU **KNOW** I'M NOT GETTING YOU A DOG!
EASY, DAD, **EASY**! THERE'S PLENTY OF OTHER POSSIBILITIES ON MY LIST!
NUMBER TWO: A HORSE!
Peirce

DAD, WHAT SHOULD I GET ELLEN FOR CHRISTMAS?
HMM... BUYING GIFTS IS ALWAYS TOUGH, NATE....
...BUT IT HELPS TO TRY TO PUT YOURSELF IN THE OTHER PERSON'S SHOES! TRY TO THINK OF WHAT THEY MIGHT WANT OR NEED!
TRY TO IMAGINE THAT **YOU'RE** ELLEN!
SHUDDER!
Peirce

P.S. 38
6TH GRADE
CHRISTMAS
PLAY
"THE
MIRACLE
OF
CHRISTMAS"
"WHAT A BEAUTIFUL NIGHT! HOW BRIGHTLY THE STARS SHINE!"
"HOW BRIGHTLY THE STARS SHINE!"
OH! UH......"AND LOOK! ONE STAR SHINES MORE BRIGHTLY THAN THE OTHERS!"
"YES! SURELY THIS IS A WONDROUS SIGN!"
"SURELY THIS IS A WONDROUS SIGN!"
UH.... HOLD ON A SEC.....
KRINKLE
CRUMPLE
"THERE! IN THE SKY! AN ANGLE!"
THAT'S "ANGEL!"
RIGHT! THAT'S WHAT I MEANT!
THERE'S ALWAYS ONE WHO RUINS IT FOR ALL THE OTHERS!
WHOSE KID IS THAT?

I JUST **WUV** CHWISTMAS! DON'T YOU, SNUFFLES?
WOOF!
YEESH!
Peirce
THESE CHRISTMAS SHOWS ON TV ARE THE WORST! THEY'RE ALL SO SAPPY AND STUPID!
KLIK!
BY GOLLY, I'M GOING TO WRITE MY **OWN** CHRISTMAS SPECIAL! I'LL SHOW THESE TV PEOPLE HOW IT'S DONE!
A DR. CESSPOOL CHRISTMAS!
♪ Dashing through the snow... Tra La La La LA....
HELP!

A DR. CESSPOOL CHRISTMAS!
Christmas Eve at the hospital:
Jingle bells Jingle bells Scoobie doobie doo...
Hello Doctor! Are you going out to cut down a Christmas tree?
Nurse Maureen Biology
A Christmas tree? No, why do you ask?
Well... You're carrying a chainsaw.
Of COURSE I'm carrying a chainsaw, you nimrod! I'm on my way to SURGERY!
I... I'm SORRY, Doctor!
ORDERLY! Prepare Mrs. Gruber for her tummy tuck!
VROOM! VROOM!
continued!

READ ON, DAD! "A DOCTOR CESSPOOL CHRISTMAS" GETS BETTER AND BETTER!
"AS OUR STORY CONTINUES, IT IS CHRISTMAS EVE IN THE HOSPITAL EMERGENCY ROOM..."
Peirce
You say this poor devil was found stuck in a CHIMNEY?
Yes, Doctor, and.. EGAD! LOOK at him!!
The white beard! The bright red suit! The shiny black boots! The cap with a pom-pom! DOCTOR! Do you know who this IS??
Evidently someone with absolutely NO fashion sense!!
continued!

A DR. CESSPOOL CHRISTMAS (cont'd.)
Dr. Cesspool has just performed surgery on SANTA CLAUS!!
He's waking up, Doctor!
He IS?? Gee, that almost NEVER happens!
Thanks for saving my life, Doc!
Hey, my pleasure, Santa!
Let me tell you... I've performed a lot of operations in my time, but THIS one was pretty hairy!
You mean... the surgery almost wasn't successful?
No, I mean it was HAIRY!! Invest in a razor, for pete's sake!

A Dr. Cesspool CHRISTMAS!! (continued)
Thanks for the surgery, Doc! Now I can deliver all my gifts!
No problemo, Santa!
You might say you operated on me in the "NICK" of time! HA! HA!
Santa, you SLEIGH me!
"SLEIGH ME!" GET IT?
I GET IT.
DO I CRACK MYSELF UP OR WHAT?
CONSIDER YOURSELF CRACKED.
Peirce

HERE'S RUDOLPH THE RED-NOSED REINDEER DASHING THROUGH THE SNOW ON CHRISTMAS EVE!...
BUT OH NO! HERE COMES A GIANT ASTEROID HURTLING OUT OF THE SKY!
LOOK OUT!
WHAM!
I LOVE MAKING CHRISTMAS COOKIES...
ARE YOU THROUGH KNEADING THE DOUGH?
Peirce

WHAT'S IN THE BAG?
MY CHRISTMAS PRESENT FOR DAD!
DAD'S REALLY HARD TO BUY STUFF FOR, DON'T YOU THINK?
I MEAN, IT'S NOT LIKE HE GOES AROUND DROPPING HINTS OR ANYTHING!
I TRY TO ASK MYSELF: "IF I WERE DAD, WHAT WOULD I WANT?"
"IS THERE ANYTHING DAD REALLY NEEDS? ANYTHING I CAN BUY THAT WILL MAKE HIS LIFE EASIER?"
YOU'RE ASKING YOURSELF THE WRONG QUESTIONS, ELLEN! YOU SHOULD TRY MY APPROACH!
I ASK MYSELF: "IF DAD DOESN'T LIKE THIS GIFT, IS IT SOMETHING I CAN USE?"
MERRY CHRISTMAS.
HERE, HELP ME WRAP THIS.

PLINK!
PLONK!
OH NO...
PLINK!
PLUNK!
CHESTNUTS ROASTING ON AN OPEN FIIIIRE......
I CAN'T TAKE IT.
PLONK!
Peirce

JINGLE BELLS.... JINGLE BELLS.... JINGLE ALL THE WAAAAAY....
PLINK!
HMM..... THE FIRE'S GETTING LOW.....
...AND WE'RE ALL OUT OF KINDLING.
MAY I MAKE A FABULOUS SUGGESTION?
YOU MAY NOT!
PEIRCE

DAD! HEY DAD! WAKE UP!
IT'S CHRISTMAS, DAD! WAKE UP! IT'S CHRISTMAS!
BOUNCE! BOUNCE!
NATE, IT'S FIVE A.M.!!
FIVE A.M.?
DANG! I OVER-SLEPT!
CLOSE THE DOOR ON YOUR WAY OUT.
Peirce

'Twas the day after Christmas
And inside the house
Ellen was wearing
a real ugly blouse.
HEL-LO!
$12.99 from "House O' Blouse"
Dad had been given
some weights as a gift
And was trying (and failing)
to give them a lift.
OOF!
CRACK!
Christmas is over.
Of that there's no question
And Dad's home-cooked dinner
caused much indigestion.
TA-DA!
So 'til next December
Discard all those yule lists
And remember this lesson:
BIG NATE is the coolest!
HAPPY HOLIDAYS!

I HAVE THE "POST-CHRISTMAS BLUES."
I UNDERSTAND COMPLETELY!
FOR MONTHS YOU LOOKED FORWARD TO CHRISTMAS! THAT ONE DAY WAS THE FOCUS OF ALL YOUR ATTENTION! AND NOW IT'S OVER!
YOU NO LONGER HAVE CHRISTMAS TO LOOK FORWARD TO! YOU FEEL DEPRIVED OF THE EXCITEMENT, THE HAPPINESS, THE WARMTH! ISN'T THAT RIGHT?
NO, I JUST DIDN'T GET ALL THE PRESENTS I WANTED.
Peirce

WELL, DAD, CHRISTMAS IS OVER!
YUP.
ANOTHER HOLIDAY COME AND GONE!
MM-HMM....
WELL, ENOUGH SMALL TALK! HERE'S MY LIST FOR NEXT CHRISTMAS!
YOU'LL NOTICE I'VE HIGH-LIGHTED THE ITEMS YOU DIDN'T GET ME **THIS** YEAR!
Peirce

HAVE YOU FINISHED YOUR "THANK-YOU" LETTER TO AUNT EDNA?
NO.... I CAN'T THINK OF WHAT TO WRITE.
JUST WRITE WHAT COMES NATURALLY! JUST BE YOURSELF!
THAT'S THE MOST IMPORTANT THING, NATE: BE YOURSELF!
Dear Aunt Edna:
Thank you for the shirt you gave me for Christmas. Blue is my favorite color. I guess the shirt you gave me isn't exactly blue, though. It is more like a gross purple.
Anyway, you should see the sweater Ellen got. It is big and brown. When she wears it, she looks like a giant mole. (HA HA)
Speaking of moles, how is the one on your face?
Well, that's all for now. Thanks again for the shirt. It is good to have something to wear in case all my nice clothes are being washed or something.
HAPPY NEW YEAR!
You
Love, Nate
I'M DONE!
LET ME SEE.
NATE, REMEMBER WHEN I TOLD YOU TO JUST BE YOURSELF?
YEAH?
BE SOMEONE ELSE.

COME ON IN, FRANCIS! READY FOR OUR NEW YEAR'S EVE SLEEP-OVER?
YEAH!
THIS WILL BE A BLAST! WE CAN POP POPCORN AND PLAY "MONOPOLY"!
THEN LATER WE CAN WATCH THE COUNTDOWN TO NEW YEAR'S ON TV!
THEN WHAT HAPPENS?
WE MAKE RESOLUTIONS, AND THEN BREAK THEM!
AWESOME!
PEIRCE

WATCHING THE COUNT-DOWN ON TV ?
YUP!
THIRTY SECONDS TO NEW YEAR'S!.... **TWENTY** SECONDS!
TEN!
ISN'T IT TRADITIONAL TO SMOOCH AT MIDNIGHT?
PEIRCE

Big Nate is distributed internationally by Universal Uclick.

Andrews McMeel Publishing
a division of Andrews McMeel Universal
1130 Walnut Street, Kansas City, Missouri 64106

www.andrewsmcmeel.com

16 17 18 19 20 SDB 10 9 8 7 6 5 4 3 2 1

ISBN: 978-1-4494-8200-8

These strips appeared in newspapers from
September 8, 1991, through December 31, 1991.

Big Nate can be viewed on the Internet at
www.gocomics.com/big_nate

amp! COMICS for kids

Check out these and other books at ampkids.com

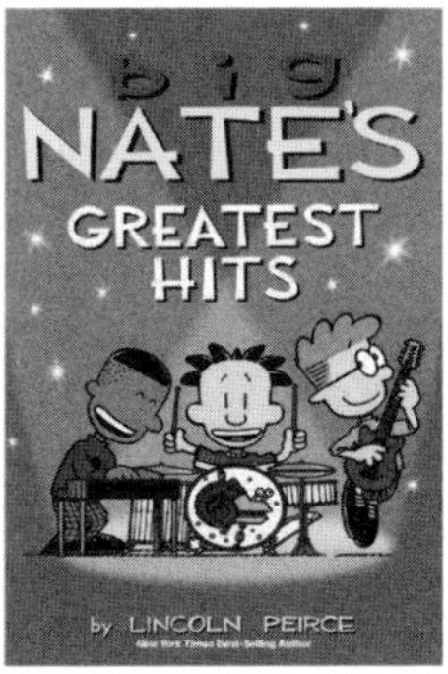

Also available:
Teaching and activity guides for each title.
AMP! Comics for Kids books make reading FUN!